Kathe

MW00614706

Contents

Introduction 1

Part 1   **Action Songs** 7
"Bingo" 8
"You Must Come in at the Door" 9
Theme from _The New World Symphony_ 9
"Shoo Fly" 10
"Twinkle, Twinkle Little Star" 11
"Take Me Out to the Ball Game" 12
"Put Your Hand in the Air" 13
"The Missouri Waltz" 14
"Jitterboogie" 14
"This Is the Way" 15
"Looby Lou" 16
"Mary Ann McCarthy" 17
"Mama Don't 'Low" 18

Part 2   **Songs for Successful Sing-Alongs** 21
"Daisy Bell" 22
"By the Light of the Silvery Moon" 24
"Take Me Out to the Ball Game" 26
"Amazing Grace" 28
"Ja-Da" 30
"After the Ball" 32
"Oh! Susanna" 34

"The Sidewalks of New York" 36
"Swing Low, Sweet Chariot" 38
"Aba Daba Honeymoon" 40
"Shine On, Harvest Moon" 42
"You're A Grand Old Flag" 44
"Peg O' My Heart" 46
"Meet Me in St. Louis, Louis" 48
"I Want a Girl" 50
"Yankee Doodle Boy" 52
"America, the Beautiful" 54
"School Days" 56
"For Me and My Gal" 58
"Let Me Call You Sweetheart" 60

Part 3   **Music for Reminiscing** 63
"It's Been a Long Long Time" 66
"I Don't Know Why I Love You Like I Do" 66
"You Are My Sunshine" 67
"Mairzy Doats (and Doazy Doats)" 68
"Honey" 68
"Oh, Johnny, Oh" 69
"I Don't Want to Set the World on Fire
      (I Just Want to Start a Flame in Your Heart)" . . 70
"You Made Me Love You" 70
"Oh What A Beautiful Morning!" 71
"Let It Snow! Let It Snow! Let It Snow!" 71

Quizzes 72
Anecdotes 82

Audiocassette Song Sequence 92

INTRODUCTION

I f referring to music as a "universal language" is a cliché,
it is a cliché rooted deeply in truth. The universality of
music transcends cultural differences, age, and levels of
awareness. When carefully and sensitively selected, music activities may be shared by older adults who remain intel-
lectually alert and by older people whose intellectual faculties
have diminished.

That is what I have attempted to do in this book. I did
not set out to create an all-purpose music activities tape and
text, but the focus changed upon observing that older adults
at adult day care centers, senior centers, and long-term care
facilities display a wide variety of cognitive abilities. These ex-
periences led me to develop music activities that stimulate
everyone, regardless of cognitive level.

Dementia *un*focuses the mind; it makes it difficult or im-
possible to follow the paths of thought normally taken for
granted. A striking attribute of music is its ability to connect
with people with dementia when all other forms of stimula-

1

tion have been unsuccessful. Rhythm can insinuate itself into older people, who spontaneously start clapping, tapping their toes, or swaying with the music. Even more sophisticated musical abilities are retained by people with dementia. These people still possess the ability to sing on pitch and to remember the lyrics of old songs.

Dr. Oliver Sacks, a well-known neurologist and the author of *Awakenings*, has noted that people who can no longer use or understand language and cannot achieve conceptual thought often respond to music. "I've seen patients who couldn't take a single step but could dance, and patients who could not utter a single syllable but could sing" (*Washington Post Health Supplement*, July 5, 1994).

In my work with older people with dementia, I occasionally play a 1940s recording of "You Are My Sunshine," and nearly always, most participants sing along. When I play the song on the piano, the room fills with the smiles that happy memories bring. Similarly, when I play the swing era favorite "Sentimental Journey," and sometimes mischievously insert a few bars of "Pop Goes the Weasel" at the end of the song's bridge, a chuckle or two usually rises from the audience. The complex mechanism that makes certain things humorous because they are non sequitur continues to function, even in people with dementia.

All available data reveal that music is a remarkably effective vehicle for sensory stimulation. If music cannot break through the barriers placed in front of a confused mind, chances are little else will. Music improves concentration, motivates the spirit, calms the soul, and enhances self-esteem.

Alice Ann Clair, director of music therapy at The University of Kansas, finds that music, with its built-in structure, helps bring some semblance of order to lives affected by dementia. Clair states, "Rhythm provides structure and security.

It's anxiety reducing. We found very early that people who bump into others and wander around will easily sit still for 30 minutes with some music" (*Washington Post Health Supplement*, July 5, 1994).

Although music activity may temporarily restore focus, it is still found, with some frustration, that such activity does not reach all the participants in a group, particularly older people who are severely withdrawn. I have used the technique of sound amplification to some benefit with these people. A curious phenomenon occurs when the activity director at a facility electronically amplifies his or her normal speaking voice. Provided the amplification is *moderately* loud, members of the group who were previously unfocused may suddenly begin to focus on the voice that, to them, has mysteriously interrupted their solitude. In addition, older people who usually mumble or whisper often sing quite clearly when startled into hearing their own voices electronically amplified. The microphone can be an invaluable device in a group of people with depression or in a group of people in the advanced stages of Alzheimer's disease.

The music activities and the audiotape were designed to be used by activity directors with little or no musical background, by music specialists, or by older adults in their homes. The section of action songs (Part 1) contains selections that have worked best with participants coping with Alzheimer's disease and related dementias; but "Bingo," "You Must Come in at the Door," "Put Your Hand in the Air," "Jitterboogie," "Mary Ann McCarthy," and "Mama Don't 'Low" have brought laughter as well as needed exercise to hundreds of healthy older adults in the music activities programs.

Part 2 of this book contains 18 songs with equal appeal and accessibility to persons with dementia and to healthy older adults. The leader can either sing along with the music tape (on the tape the words are called out ahead of time so the participants do not need to know the words or to read them), or, if the leader plays a guitar, chord organ, piano, keyboard, or other instrument, he or she can accompany the song. The reader with some musical background may notice that all the songs are notated in low-pitched keys. In general, older adults find high-pitched phrases a strain. These familiar melodies have been rewritten in a key that will encourage participants to sing along.

Each song in the sing-along section of this tape and text, Part 2, is preceded by background information on the song, which may be used by the group leader as a device to inspire conversation and reminiscing. Included are the stories behind the songs and the news events of the day in which the songs first appeared. Not all groups will be able to benefit from this historical material. Activity directors should use judgment in determining when it is appropriate to use this material.

The material in Part 3 can be used by activity directors as an interlude when a group's attention begins to lag. I have found in my work with older adults that a group's attention can be revitalized easily by interjecting a brief, succinct story about a famous big band singer or a reminiscence about a familiar tune. Although the anecdotes and quizzes are presented together, they are meant to be "sprinkled" between songs as needed.

Many of the songs from the war years (both world wars) contain some homily or shred of not-so-unsophisticated philosophy. The craftsmanship of some of these songs raises them to the level of art; others, perhaps less artistic, have lasted, I believe, because their messages contain broadly stated truths. Typical lyrics from these old favorites are the following:

1.   "Enjoy yourself, it's later than you think."

2.   "I don't know why I love you like I do."

3. "Fortune's always hiding, I've looked everywhere; I'm forever blowing bubbles, pretty bubbles in the air."

4. "We ain't got a barrel of money…but we'll travel along, singin' a song, side by side."

5. "I want to be happy, but I won't be happy, 'til I make you happy, too."

6. "Though April showers may come your way, they bring the flowers that bloom in May."

7. "When you're smiling, the whole world smiles with you."

8. "Gee, but I'd give the world to see that old gang of mine."

9. "I'm gonna live till I die."

There seems to be a song for nearly everything we feel. The catchphrases in these songs are fully developed into a sort of psalm, which, when recited, can calm a troubled spirit.

So, it is with good reason that I have entitled this book and tape *The Power of Music*. Now the power is in your hands.

PART 1

ACTION SONGS

Action songs are songs that stimulate physical activity among members of a group of older adults. These tunes serve to sharpen dulled proprioception (reception of stimuli by an individual) skills and foster positive emotional responses.

"BINGO"

This is a song that everyone remembers from child-hood. The group leader should clap loudly at the appropriate places to encourage the participants to do the same. In some groups it is helpful to write the word *BINGO* in large capital letters on a chalkboard or poster board; as the song progresses, cross out each letter that is clapped but no longer sung. (The × over the letter indicates when the participants should clap.)

CHORUS 1

> There was a farmer had a dog
> And Bingo was his name-o
> B-I-N-G-O
> B-I-N-G-O
> B-I-N-G-O
> And Bingo was his name-o.

CHORUS 2

> There was a farmer had a dog
> And Bingo was his name-o
> X-I-N-G-O
> X-I-N-G-O
> X-I-N-G-O
> And Bingo was his name-o.

Continue singing chorus after chorus until all the letters in *BINGO* are clapped instead of sung.

"YOU MUST COME IN AT THE DOOR"

Once heard on the tape, this song will be familiar to nearly all participants. It combines physical exercise and clapping in unison at the appropriate place. At first the participants will join in singing on the chorus only, but given time, they will sing the entire song. If the activity director wishes, he or she may, without musical accompaniment, simply *recite* the chorus of this song while demonstrating relaxing stretches.

CHORUS

> So high, you can't get over it (stretch up)
> So low, you can't get under it (stretch down)
> So wide, you can't get around it (stretch out)
> You must come in at the door! (after word "door," clap, clap)

VERSE

> One of these days, about 12 o'clock
> This old world is gonna reel and rock.

THEME FROM
THE NEW WORLD SYMPHONY
(A QUIETING ACTIVITY)

Occasionally, an activity director may find it necessary to put a brake on the action to calm a group or an individual who is overly excited. This soothing melody, played on French horn, will usually do the trick.

"SHOO FLY"

This is a song *everyone* remembers; it is so simple and repetitious that even people in the later stages of Alzheimer's disease usually sing along. (Suggestion: When the words *shoo fly* appear in the lyrics, ask the participants to clap. While they are clapping on the words *shoo fly*, pretend to swat the fly.)

CHORUS

> (clap) (clap)
> Shoo, fly, don't bother me.
> (clap) (clap)
> Shoo, fly, don't bother me.
> (clap) (clap)
> Shoo, fly, don't bother me.
> For I belong to somebody.

VERSE

> I feel, I feel, I feel
> I feel like a morning star.
> I feel, I feel, I feel
> I feel like a morning star.

Repeat chorus.

"TWINKLE, TWINKLE LITTLE STAR"

This familiar tune can be sung once by the group before asking that they join the taped singing. Actions, although obvious, might bear reviewing: When the lyric "up above . . ." is sung, the leader should point upward. When the phrase "diamond in the sky" is sung, the leader should make a diamond shape, if possible, by touching thumbs together and index fingers together. Some groups may wish to join in singing, not on the entire song, but on the words "Twinkle, twinkle little star, how I wonder what you are." Most will sing the entire verse.

> Twinkle, twinkle little star,
> How I wonder what you are.
> Up above the world so high,
> Like a diamond in the sky.
> Twinkle, twinkle little star,
> How I wonder what you are.

"TAKE ME OUT
TO THE BALL GAME"

(INSTRUMENTAL)

A lthough the participants may sing if they wish, this old favorite works here primarily as an instrumental for movement with music.

> Take me out to the ball game
> Take me out to the crowd
> Buy me some peanuts and Crackerjack
> I don't care if I never get back
> For it's *root, root, root* for the home team
> If they don't win it's a shame
> For it's *one, two, three* strikes you're out
> At the old ball game.

A variety of actions work well for this song, some of which are listed below:

1. Swing an imaginary bat at an imaginary ball (lines 1 and 2).
2. Pantomime opening a box and eating the contents (line 3).
3. Raise a fist in the air three times (line 5).
4. Clap three times (line 7).
5. Clap every first beat of this fast waltz (1 2 3, 1 2 3).
6. Sway.
7. Do any or all of the above—this is a song that easily stimulates action.

"PUT YOUR HAND IN THE AIR"

(NEW WORDS AND MUSIC BY BILL MESSENGER)

A sk the group to follow the movements indicated in the song. By the second hearing, the group will, without any encouragement, find themselves singing along.

VERSES

Put your hands in the air, in the air. (Repeat)
Put your hands in the air,
You can *clap* 'em while they're there.
Put your hands in the air, in the air.

Hold the hand of a friend, hold a hand.
(Repeat)
Hold the hand of a friend,
If you're happy, say *"Amen."*
Hold the hand of a friend, hold a hand.

Lift a foot in the air, in the air. (Repeat)
Lift a foot in the air,
And pretend you're Fred Astaire.
Lift a foot in the air, in the air.

Raise your body in the air, in the air. (Repeat)
Raise your body in the air,
Now return it to your chair.
Raise your body in the air, in the air.

Clap along as you sing, as you sing. (Repeat)
Clap along as you sing,
Like a birdie on the wing.
Clap along, clap along, now *stop!*

"THE MISSOURI WALTZ"

A sweeping, romantic, sentimental song, "The Missouri Waltz" has a strong beat that is easy to dance to alone or with a partner. Most participants will enjoy dancing to this music; people who do not wish to dance may enjoy clapping as the music plays.

The most satisfying way to clap the waltz beat is in a 1, 2, 3 rhythm, with a strong accent on the "1," as was done in the "Take Me Out to the Ball Game" activity. Because the beat is far from subtle, no one should have difficulty hearing the music and clapping on the accented beat. (Variation: clap rest rest; clap rest rest.)

Dance steps do not need to follow a formal pattern, and formal etiquette can be ignored. Simply move to the music!

"JITTERBOOGIE"

(©1994 BILL MESSENGER)

Everything previously stated about "The Missouri Waltz" applies to "Jitterboogie"; the only difference is that this piece of music is a lively jitterbug instead of a romantic waltz. Grab a partner's hand and, as bandleader Kay Kyser used to say, "Let's dance, chillen!"

"THIS IS THE WAY"
(TO THE TUNE OF "HERE WE GO 'ROUND THE MULBERRY BUSH")

Tell participants that this is a song they will remember singing when they were children. Ask participants to listen to the tape and to mimic your actions. They may also sing along.

> This is the way we wash our hands, wash our
>   hands, wash our hands,
> This is the way we wash our hands,
> Early in the morning.
>
> This is the way we brush our teeth, brush our
>   teeth, brush our teeth,
> This is the way we brush our teeth,
> Early in the morning.
>
> This is the way we comb our hair, comb our
>   hair, comb our hair,
> This is the way we comb our hair,
> Early in the morning.

If you are willing to act a little silly with this verse, your participants may howl with laughter.

> This is the way we put on our clothes, put on
>   our clothes, put on our clothes,
> This is the way we put on our clothes,
> Early in the morning.

"LOOBY LOU"
(TRADITIONAL APPALACHIAN DANCE SONG)

Follow the directions on the tape for the verses. For the chorus, the group may hold hands in a circle, raising and lowering their hands or their arms in unison with the leader. If making a circle is impractical, each participant may put hands on waist and wave from side to side rhythmically.

CHORUS

> Here we go looby loo,
> Here we go looby lai,
> Here we go looby loo,
> All on a Saturday night.

VERSES

1. I put my right hand in,
   I put my right hand out,
   I put my right hand in,
   And I shake it all about.

2. I put my left hand in,
   I put my left hand out,
   I put my left hand in,
   And I shake it all about.

3. I put my right foot in,
   I put my right foot out,
   I put my right foot in,
   And I shake it all about.

4. I put my left foot in,
   I put my left foot out,
   I put my left foot in,
   And I shake it all about.

5. I put my whole self in,
   I put my whole self out,
   I put my whole self in,
   And I shake it all about.

"MARY ANN McCARTHY"
(TO THE TUNE OF "BATTLE HYMN OF THE REPUBLIC")

This is a delightfully silly parody of a classic American tune. Because the words are repetitious, the group can sing them after listening to the tape once. The activity director should lead the simple two-beat clapping pattern that appears once at the end of the verse and once at the end of the chorus.

VERSE

Mary Ann McCarthy went a-fishin' for some clams.
Mary Ann McCarthy went a-fishin' for some clams.
Mary Ann McCarthy went a-fishin' for some clams,
But she didn't get a (clap, clap) clam.

CHORUS

All she got was influenza.
All she got was influenza.
All she got was influenza,
But she didn't get a (clap, clap) clam!

"MAMA DON'T 'LOW"*

This is a Dixieland jazz standard that I have altered into an action song.

Mama don't 'low no song singin' 'round here.
Mama don't 'low no song singin' 'round here.
We don't care what mama 'low, gonna sing
   them songs any old how.
Mama don't 'low song singin' 'round here.

Mama don't 'low no hand clappin' 'round
   here.
Mama don't 'low no hand clappin' 'round
   here.
We don't care what mama 'low, gonna sing
   them songs any old how.
Mama don't 'low hand clappin' 'round here.

Mama don't 'low no finger snappin' 'round
   here.
Mama don't 'low no finger snappin' 'round
   here.
We don't care what mama 'low, gonna sing
   them songs any old how.
Mama don't 'low finger snappin' 'round here.

Mama don't 'low no high stretchin' 'round
   here.
Mama don't 'low no high stretchin' 'round
   here.

We don't care what mama 'low, gonna sing
   them songs any old how.
Mama don't 'low high stretchin' 'round here.

Mama don't 'low no foot stompin' 'round
   here.
Mama don't 'low no foot stompin' 'round
   here.
We don't care what mama 'low, gonna sing
   them songs any old how.
Mama don't 'low foot stompin' 'round here.

Mama don't 'low no song singin' 'round here.
Mama don't 'low no song singin' 'round here.
We don't care what mama 'low, gonna sing
   them songs any old how.
Mama don't 'low song singin' 'round here.

* 'Low rhymes with "cow."

Part 2

Songs for Successful

Sing-Alongs

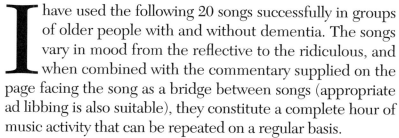

I have used the following 20 songs successfully in groups of older people with and without dementia. The songs vary in mood from the reflective to the ridiculous, and when combined with the commentary supplied on the page facing the song as a bridge between songs (appropriate ad libbing is also suitable), they constitute a complete hour of music activity that can be repeated on a regular basis.

Where appropriate, the words are shouted out ahead of time on the tape to aid the participants in singing. The songs have all been lowered in pitch to make them easier to sing.

So that this material is useful to music therapists and music activities specialists, as well as to activity directors without musical background, I have included musical notation and words.

Henry Decker was an Englishman who emigrated to the United States in 1892. Henry wanted to make a name for himself in show business, but he thought it would never happen with such an ordinary name. Thus, "Harry Dacre" was born, and with him, a show business career.

To travel around New York City to sell his songs, Dacre used the bicycle he brought with him from England. Bicycles, as a recreational vehicle, were becoming immensely popular in the "Gay 90s" both in the United States and in Europe. When Dacre told his friend, American songwriter Billy Jerome, that he had to pay a very expensive duty on his bicycle when he reached U.S. Customs, Jerome replied, "You're lucky you didn't have a *tandem* bicycle; they'd have made you pay *twice* as much."

Dacre laughed and said, "With a bicycle built for two, you could tour the countryside on your honeymoon."

Jerome said, "I dare you to turn that idea into a song."

Daisy Bell

Words by Harry Dacre

Music by Harry Dacre
Arrangement by Bill Messenger

Dai - sy, Dai - sy, give me your
Mich - ael, Mich - ael, here is your

ans - wer true, I'm half - cra -
ans - wer true, - - - - I'm not cra -

zy all for the love of you. It
zy o - ver the likes of you! If

won't be a sty - lish mar - riage for I can't af -
you can't af - ford a car - riage, there won't be

ford a car - riage. But you'll look sweet up -
an - y mar - riage. For I'll be damned if

on the seat of a bi - cy - cle built for two.
I'll be crammed on a bi - cy - cle built for two.

23

The year this song appeared, 1909, Teddy Roosevelt turned over the presidency to his handpicked successor, William Howard Taft. The "Rough Rider" immediately left the United States with his son Kermit for a hunting trip in East Africa.

Admiral Robert Peary, his African-American companion Matthew "Matt" Henson, and four unnamed Eskimos planted the U.S. flag on the North Pole. Some claim it was actually Henson, and not Peary, who was the first to set foot in the cold sunlight of the Arctic on the northernmost point of the planet Earth.

The Gibson Girl, with her plumed hat and cherry blossom lips, was still the vogue, and the latest fashion for "ladies" was the hobble skirt.

By The Light of The Silvery Moon

Words by Edward Madden

Music by Gus Edwards
Arrangement by Bill Messenger

By the light - - - of the sil-ver-y moon,

I want to spoon, To my hon-ey I'll croon love's

tune. Hon-ey - moon; keep a-shin-ing in June;

Your sil-v'ry beams will bring love dreams, We'll be cud - ling

soon, By the sil - ver-y moon.

Although it is hard to believe, it is claimed that neither the composer nor the lyricist had ever seen a baseball game before they wrote this song. If the story is true, Jack Norworth, the lyricist, must have had a vivid imagination because the details he placed in this song perfectly recreate the excitement in the stands.

This song appears in a higher-pitched and faster version in Part 1. The following version is more suitable for singing.

Take Me Out to the Ball Game

Words by Jack Norworth

Music by Albert Von Tilzer
Arrangement by Bill Messenger

T his peaceful song first appeared around 1835 and has remained a favorite hymn of people of all faiths. The melody is hauntingly beautiful.

"Amazing Grace" can be listened to or hummed if the words present too great a challenge for the group. Singing this song tends to create a feeling of quiet contentment.

Amazing Grace

Traditional
Arrangement by Bill Messenger

This bouncy tune was one of the favorite American songs of the early days of World War I. When President Woodrow Wilson announced that Prohibition was to begin on July 1, 1919, the entire country sang the following lyrics to the melody of "Ja-Da":

> Have a, have a
> Have a little drink on me.
> Have a, have a
> Have a little drink on me.
> Come on, boys, and quench your thirst;
> The county will be dry as of July 1st.
> Have a, have a
> Have a little drink on me.

Ja-Da

Words by Bob Carleton

Music by Bob Carleton
Arrangement by Bill Messenger

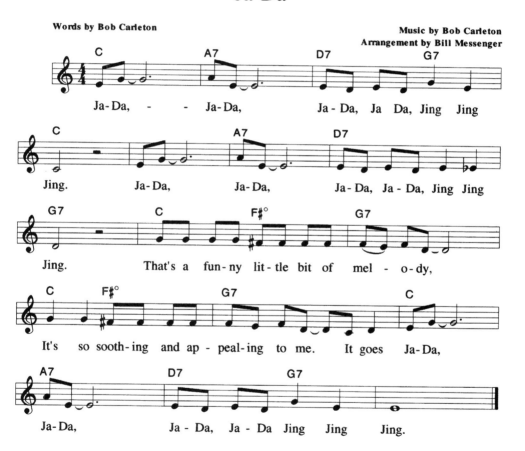

In 1880 Charles K. Harris attended a formal dance at an elegant establishment in New York City. Early in the evening, he saw a handsome young couple walking arm-in-arm. The carefully attired man was accompanied by a beautiful but seemingly shy young woman. Later the same evening, Harris saw the young man walking out of the room with a different woman on his arm. Surprised, Harris looked around the room for the first woman. He soon found her in the corner, tears streaming down her cheeks. This emotional sight inspired Harris to write "After the Ball."

"After the Ball" became the sensational hit of 1882, and the first song ever to sell 1 million copies of sheet music.

After The Ball

Words by Charles Harris

Music by Charles Harris
Arrangement by Bill Messenger

33

S tephen Foster was paid a few dollars for the rights to this song. His publishers made at least $10,000 from the song during its first decade of existence. "Oh, Susanna" was America's most popular song in 1848, and it was sung in every mining camp and hamlet in the American West during the gold rush of 1849.

Oh! Susanna

Words by Stephen C. Foster

Music by Stephen C. Foster
Arrangement by Bill Messenger

Oh I come from Al - a - ba - ma with my
rained all day the night I left, the

ban - jo on my knee, I'm going to Louis - i -
weath - er it was dry, The sun so hot I

an - a my true love for to see. It
froze to death, Su - san - na don't you cry. - - -

Oh! Su - san - na, Oh don't you cry for me, For I

come from Al - a - bam - a with my ban - jo on my knee.

35

Lottie Gibson, a diminutive beauty with a powerful voice, was the Barbra Streisand of her day (1896). As with Streisand, the public was willing to pay almost any price to hear her sing. She possessed such drawing power that newspapers called her "The Little Magnet."

This song failed when it was first introduced. With Lottie Gibson's promotion of the song, it became the number one song in America and was used by Jimmy Walker in his successful bid for mayor of New York City in 1926.

The Sidewalks of New York

Words by Charles Lawlor

Music by James Blake
Arrangement by Bill Messenger

37

This old spiritual is ideal for people with dementia because they can easily join in the singing on the audiotape on the words "comin' for to carry me home." After groups are encouraged to sing this phrase, they soon begin singing longer sections, if not the entire song.

Swing Low, Sweet Chariot

Spiritual
Arrangement by Bill Messenger

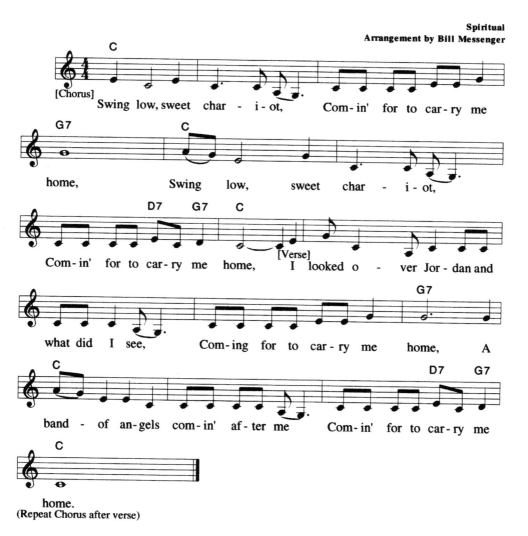

[Chorus]
Swing low, sweet char - i - ot, Com- in' for to car-ry me home, Swing low, sweet char - i - ot, Com- in' for to car-ry me home, [Verse] I looked o - ver Jor - dan and what did I see, Com- ing for to car- ry me home, A band - of an-gels com-in' af - ter me Com- in' for to car-ry me home.

(Repeat Chorus after verse)

39

Debbie Reynolds sang this silly 1914 hit in her movie debut, the 1950 musical *Two Weeks with Love*. Petite Debbie sang the song with 6'6" song and dance man Carleton Carpenter. This delightfully foolish song turned what would have been a cinematic flop into a moderately successful film.

Participants will enjoy trying to keep up with the taped singer as she sings "Aba Daba Daba Daba" faster and faster.

The Aba Daba Honeymoon

Words by Arthur Fields & Walter Donovan

Music by Arthur Fields & Walter Donovan
Arrangement by Bill Messenger

dab - a, dab - a, dab" means - Monk I love but you.

"Bab - a, dab - a, dab," in mon - key talk, means

Chimp I love you too. Then the big ba - boon one

night in June, he mar - ried them and

ver - y soon they went up - on their

ab - a, dab - a hon - ey - moon.

Nora Bayes (née Dora Goldberg) was the most popular female performer in the years immediately preceding World War I. Performing long before the development of the modern microphone, she had a booming voice that could be heard in the rear of a crowded theater or could communicate the shy and slightly naughty (for its day) mood of "Shine On, Harvest Moon," which she wrote with her husband, Jack Norworth, in 1908.

Bayes also introduced the biggest hit of 1917, George M. Cohan's "Over There."

Shine On, Harvest Moon

Words and Music by Nora Bayes & Jack Norworth
Arrangement by Bill Messenger

Shine on, shine on har-vest moon, up in the sky, I ain't had no lov - in' since Jan - u-ar - y, Feb - ru-ar - y, June and Ju - ly, Snow time ain't no time to sit out-side and spoon, So shine on, shine on har-vest moon, for me and my Gal.

By 1906 America was caught up in a frenzy of flag waving and patriotism. Teddy Roosevelt's "Big Stick" diplomacy was expanding American influence around the globe. George M. Cohan, the son of Irish immigrants, was the star of the Broadway musical *George Washington, Jr.* "You're A Grand Old Flag" was the hit song from that show.

Few of the group participants will have seen George M. Cohan in person, but they probably have seen Jimmy Cagney's award-winning performance as Cohan in the 1942 motion picture *Yankee Doodle Dandy*.

You're A Grand Old Flag

Words by George M. Cohan

Music by George M. Cohan
Arrangement by Bill Messenger

You're a grand old flag, You're a high fly - ing flag, and for - ev - er in peace may you wave. You're the em - blem of the land I love, the home of the free and the brave. Ev - 'ry heart beats true 'neath the Red, White and Blue, where there's nev - er a boast or brag But should old ac - quaint-ance be for - got, keep your eye on the grand old flag.

"Peg O' My Heart" is a song with a long and successful history. Inspired by the 1912 play of the same name, Fred Fisher wrote the song for the Ziegfeld Follies of 1913. It was an instant hit. (Laurette Taylor, the star of the play *Peg O' My Heart,* also originated the role of the mother in the Broadway production of Tennessee Williams' "The Glass Menagerie.")

In 1933 "Peg O' My Heart" became the title song of a Hollywood musical. In 1947 the Harmonicats sold several million copies of this song to make it one of the hits of that year. In 1950 the Three Suns were awarded a gold record for their recording of the song, and, during the same year, Peggy Lee's rendition of "Peg O' My Heart" nearly went gold. The song is truly a perennial.

Peg O' My Heart

Words by Alfred Bryan

Music by Fred Fisher
Arrangement by Bill Messenger

Peg o' my heart, I love you,

Don't let us part, I love you, I al - ways knew,

it would be you, Since I heard your lilt - ing laugh - ter,

it's your I - rish heart I'm af - ter. Peg o' my heart,

your glan - ces make my heart say

"How's chan - ces?" Come be my own,

Come, make your home in my heart.

47

"Meet Me in St. Louis, Louis" was the theme song of the World's Fair of 1903, a risqué event that included belly dancer Little Egypt doing the "hoochee koochee" dance in pseudo-Egyptian attire. Sigmund Spaeth, one of America's great musicologists, once suggested that the song's number one distinction is that it contains the world's worst rhyme—"hoochee koochee"/"tootsie wootsie."

The song enjoyed a revival during the first run of the 1944 MGM film musical of the same name starring Judy Garland and Margaret O'Brien.

Meet Me In St. Louis, Louis

Words by Andrew Sterling

Music by Kerry Mills
Arrangement by Bill Messenger

49

Harry Von Tilzer, the composer of "I Want a Girl," bought the title from a friend who thought it would be amusing to create a song that had the world's longest title. The complete title on the original sheet music is "I Want a Girl Just Like the Girl Who Married Dear Old Dad." Irving Berlin later went Von Tilzer one better by writing a song called "How Could You Believe Me When I Said I Love You When You Know I've Been a Liar All My Life?" Then, in the 1930s, Ozzie Nelson recorded what remains the world's longest song title: "I'm Looking For a Guy Who Plays Alto and Tenor Sax and Doubles on Clarinet and Wears a Size 37 Suit."

I Want A Girl

Words by William Dillon

Music by Harry Von Tilzer
Arrangement by Bill Messenger

I want a girl, just like the girl that mar-ried dear old Dad.

She was a pearl, and the on-ly girl that Dad-dy ev-er had.

Good old - fash-ioned girl with heart so true;

One who loved no-bod-y else but you, - I want a girl,

just like the girl that mar-ried dear old Dad.

This old favorite is another of George M. Cohan's patriotic songs. Although Cohan claimed he was born on the fourth of July, he was actually born on July 3.

Yankee Doodle Boy

Words by George M. Cohan

Music by George M. Cohan
Arrangement by Bill Messenger

I'm a Yan-kee Doo-dle Dan - dy, A Yan-kee Doo-dle, do or die. A real live neph-ew of my Un - cle Sam, Born on the fourth of Ju-ly. I've got a Yan-kee Doo-dle sweet - heart, She's my Yan-kee-Doo-dle joy, Yan-kee Doo-dle came to Lon-don just to ride the pon - ies, I am a Yan-kee Doo-dle Boy.

"America, the Beautiful" is one of the loveliest and most enduring tributes to the United States in song. Still, people have always been puzzled by the line "Thine alabaster cities gleam," from the second verse. American cities were then constructed from dark-colored stone or wood, all except for the model city at the 1893 World's Columbian Exposition in Chicago. The walls were not true alabaster (white marble), but a newly introduced material called "plywood," covered with plaster. Visitors to the Exposition were certain they were looking at marble until they touched one of these "alabaster" walls. The illusion was incredible—an endless city of white palaces.

One of the stunned spectators was Katherine Lee Bates, composer of "America, the Beautiful." So moved by the sight of the "alabaster" palaces, Mrs. Bates wrote the second verse to this patriotic song in less than half an hour. (The first verse was inspired by an earlier trip to Pike's Peak.)

America, The Beautiful

Words by Katherine Lee Bates

Music by Samuel A. Ward
Arrangement by Bill Messenger

2. Oh beautiful for patriot dream
That sees beyond the years,
Thine alabaster cities gleam,
Undimmed by human tears.
America, America,
God shed his grace on thee,
And crown thy good with brotherhood,
From sea to shining sea.

This song originated in 1907 in Gus Edwards' "School Days" (sometimes spelled "School Daze") vaudeville act. Edwards played the harried teacher of a classroom full of young cutups and clowns. The following is an actual segment of a sketch from the original script.

Teacher: Chuckie, take your feet off the desk.
Chuck: It's my desk, ain't it?
Teacher: Yes.
Chuck: Well, what do you want?
Teacher: I want you to take your feet off that desk.
Chuck: Now let me tell you something, Teach. You know my Dad pays taxes to keep this school running, and the people pay your salary; I *am* the people. You'll admit that you are a public servant?
Teacher: [Exasperated] Yes, I am a public servant.
Chuck: Well, get me a glass of water.

If the mood of the group is right, it can be fun to ask two people to play the teacher and Chuck and act out the script before leading the group in song.

The activity director may also want to read the following Prohibition-era parody of "School Days" to the group:

> School days, school days,
> Poker, dice, and pool days.
> Necking and wrecking and how to be fast,
> Taught to the tune of a hip pocket flask.
> You were my queen with dress cut low,
> I was your half-shot Romeo.
> You wrote on my slate,
> "You're too darned slow!"
> When we were a couple of kids.

School Days

Words by Will Cobb

Music by Gus Edwards
Arrangement by Bill Messenger

57

When "For Me and My Gal" first appeared, in 1916, America was experiencing a time of strong antiwar sentiment. Composers produced songs such as "I Didn't Raise My Boy to Be a Soldier." America was resisting involvement in World War I, but President Wilson did not live up to his campaign promise to "keep us out of war."

The top film stars were dark-eyed vamp Theda Bara (formerly Theodosia Goodman of the Bronx) and Charlie Chaplin, and other than this song, the top songs of 1916 were "Twelfth Street Rag," "Poor Butterfly," "Nola," "I Ain't Got Nobody," and "Pretty Baby."

For Me and My Gal

Words by Edgar Leslie & E. Ray Goetz

Music by George Meyer
Arrangement by Bill Messenger

The bells are ring - ing for me and my gal,

The birds are sing - ing for me and my gal.

Ev - 'ry bod - y's been know - ing, to a wed - ding they're

go - ing, and for weeks they've been sew - ing,

Ev - 'ry Sus - ie and Sal. They're con - gre - gat - ing

for me and my gal, The Par - son's wait - ing -

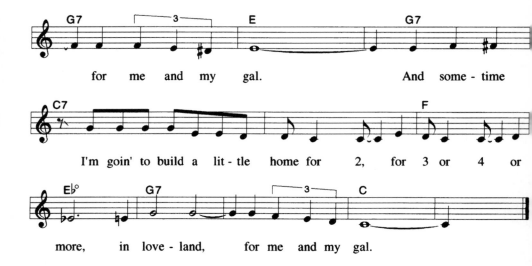

for   me   and   my   gal.   And some - time

I'm goin' to build a lit - tle   home for   2,   for 3 or   4   or

more,   in love - land,   for me and my gal.

It seems appropriate to end this part with the most re-quested of all sing-along favorites. Little can be said about this 1910 hit except that older adults of all shapes, sizes, and physical conditions love to sing this soothing, sentimental song.

Let Me Call You Sweetheart

Words by Beth Whitson

Music by Leo Friedman
Arrangement by Bill Messenger

PART 3

MUSIC FOR
REMINISCING

W hen a person has climbed to the peak of a mountain, regardless of how dizzying the height, he or she feels compelled to look down and survey the scenery left behind. By the same token, all people, regardless of age, feel the need to review where they have been, the life they have led, the people they have known.

Reminiscing is reviewing; sometimes pleasurable, sometimes painful, but nevertheless cathartic and absolutely necessary. *Cogito ergo sum*—I think, therefore I am. We reminisce, therefore we ease the burden of our later years by reassuring ourselves that we have indeed existed. We have not, as we all fear in our worst moments, somehow traveled from birth to death without savoring the life that lies between those two extremes.

The problem with most questions designed to initiate reminiscing in a group setting is that reasonably alert participants often find such questions contrived and either resist taking the journey down memory lane or make the excursion halfheartedly, passing by a chance for a deeply satisfying experience. Music, however, is such a primitive and direct stimulus that the right melody with the right associations drives itself deeply into our memory and brings back the past vividly. Each of us is moved by hearing the music that inspires us to remember a tender part of our life.

Another reason music works so well, particularly with the World War II generation, is that the popular culture of their era cut across racial, age, economical, and educational differences. They grew up with the "America is a melting pot" metaphor, which, although it may have obscured cultural differences, accentuated similarities.

In the 1940s Americans tended to embrace and "Americanize" whatever was culturally different. The Andrews Sisters' versions of a Polish dance ("Beer Barrel Polka"), a Yiddish song ("Bei Mir Bist Du Schön"), and a Maori farewell song ("Now Is the Hour") became popular around the world.

As a result, the popular music of the 1920s, 1930s, and 1940s represents a common bond for older adults. Swing era participants, regardless of race, love both Goodman and Ellington, and both Artie Shaw and Lionel Hampton. For a brief period, swing merged white and black cultures, and the results of that merger remain with us today when working with diverse groups of older adults.

One of the easiest and most natural ways of using music for reminiscing is simply to play a recording of a song that possesses strong associations for the specific age group and, after listening, to ask a few simple questions:

1. Does everyone remember that song?
2. When was it popular? Was it popular during World War II?
3. Do you remember how old you were when you first heard it? Where did you live and what were you doing in school or at work?
4. How does the song make you feel? Did you and your wife, or husband, dance to this one?
5. Would you like to sing it? Do you want to sing it with or without the record? See how much of the lyrics you can remember.

If all goes well, by the time question 5 is reached, an otherwise diverse group of older adults will have a sense of common ground because most of the group will experience a similar emotional response to the music.

The preceding questions are simple and natural, but they are only the beginning. Many more questions will grow out of the group's (or the individual's) responses and the music played. It is not so much the questions as it is the music that acts as a time machine. This kind of reminiscing is just a form of conversation; the music becomes the conversation piece. However minor an art form popular music may be, it does what all real art does—it creates order out of apparent chaos.

The following songs, quizzes, and anecdotes hold strong appeal for people born in the 1920s and 1930s, especially the musical anecdotes, particularly if recordings by the original artists are played. These recordings are not included on our tape because of copyright restrictions, but they are readily available on various albums and cassettes. The songs are simple, familiar, and repetitious enough to allow most older adults to sing along after a single listening. This material is meant to stimulate reminiscing among older adults.

"IT'S BEEN A LONG LONG TIME"

This song was one of the top 10 hits of 1945; it was number one on the Hit Parade for 5 weeks. Of the dozens of recordings made of this song, the one most people are familiar with is the Harry James recording featuring vocalist Kitty Kallen, who had a blockbuster hit in the 1950s called "Little Things Mean a Lot."

This song marks the second and most successful collaboration of Sammy Cahn and Jule Styne. Cahn went on to become Frank Sinatra's chief lyricist, penning "Teach Me Tonight," "High Hopes," "The Second Time Around," "My Kind of Town," and "Call Me Irresponsible." Styne went on to compose the scores for the Broadway musicals *Gentlemen Prefer Blondes, Gypsy, Bells Are Ringing,* and *Funny Girl.*

Variety named "It's Been A Long Long Time" as one of the top songs of the first half of the twentieth century.

"I DON'T KNOW WHY (I JUST DO)"

Roy Turk wrote the words to Fred Ahlert's melody in 1931, but this song continued to increase in popularity for the next 2 decades. As a result, most people think of this as a song of the 1940s. It was recorded by nearly every well-known swing band, but no single recording stands out as a blockbuster. It is especially good for singing, with a simple melody and easily remembered words. For the words, ask any older adult to sing the song. Chances are he or she will know it from beginning to end.

"YOU ARE MY SUNSHINE"

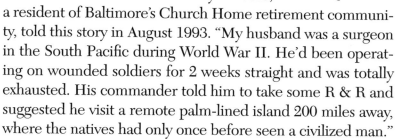

Jimmie Davis wrote this song with Charles Mitchell in 1937 and sang it to voters as he campaigned for governor of Louisiana in 1941; he was elected to two terms. Davis claims it is the most recorded popular song of all time. He is probably right because it is a simple song with universal images that have allowed it to be translated easily into almost every known language.

The following anecdote gives credence to Davis' claim. Mrs. Carolyn Moore, a resident of Baltimore's Church Home retirement community, told this story in August 1993. "My husband was a surgeon in the South Pacific during World War II. He'd been operating on wounded soldiers for 2 weeks straight and was totally exhausted. His commander told him to take some R & R and suggested he visit a remote palm-lined island 200 miles away, where the natives had only once before seen a civilized man."

The commander told Dr. Moore that he would enjoy seeing a pristine primitive society, where the customs and songs were different from anything he'd ever experienced. When he arrived on the island, a hundred naked little boys surrounded him and sang, in a combination of English and Polynesian, "You Are My Sunshine."

"MAIRZY DOATS (AND DOAZY DOATS)"

This silly hit of 1943 always brings smiles to the faces of older adults. Composer/lyricist Milton Drake got the idea for the song when his 4-year-old daughter came home from kindergarten one day talking a mile a minute. He could not understand a word, but he discovered when he calmed her down that what she was saying made sense. So "Mairzy Doats" became "mares eat oats."

"HONEY"

The song "Honey" first appeared in 1928 and, after being sung by Rudy Vallee on his radio program, sold more than 1 million copies of sheet music. Nearly every older adult recognizes the song after hearing the first five notes. One thing that makes the words to this song so easy to remember is that the name "Honey" appears in this unusually short song (16 measures instead of the usual 32) no fewer than six times.

"OH, JOHNNY, OH"

This song was written in 1917, just after America's entry into World War I. Songwriting team Abe Olman and Ed Rose originally wrote the lyric "Oh, Johnny, how you can fight!," but decided to change it to "Oh, Johnny, how you can love!"

The song was revived in 1939 by Wee Bonnie Baker recording with the Orrin Tucker big band. Once you have heard Baker's coy, little-girl voice on this recording, you never forget it.

"I DON'T WANT TO SET THE WORLD ON FIRE (I JUST WANT TO START A FLAME IN YOUR HEART)"

This is a Seiler–Marcus–Benjamin–Durham collaboration from 1941. The most memorable recording of this song was made by The Ink Spots. Baltimore-born Bill Kenny sang the melody in a high falsetto voice and was followed by the deep bass voice of his guitarist, who spoke the words over a vocal background. The Ink Spots sound is immediately identifiable to older adults.

"YOU MADE ME LOVE YOU"

This 1913 hit was introduced by Al Jolson at the Winter Garden Theatre in New York City, but the song found greater success when 15-year-old Judy Garland sang it in the film *Broadway Melody of 1938* to a framed photograph of Clark Gable. In 1941 Harry James gave the melody another boost with his million-selling recording of the song.

"OH, WHAT A BEAUTIFUL MORNING!"

As conventional as this song seems, it opened the musical *Oklahoma* in a way that was radical for 1943. Instead of opening with the usual bevy of chorus girls, *Oklahoma* began quietly with "Curly" (as played by Alfred Drake) walking on to a deserted stage to sing this gentle song alone. Composers Rodgers and Hammerstein were told that such a simple opener would never work. *Oklahoma* ran for several years on Broadway and was made into one of MGM's greatest musicals, starring Gordon MacRae as "Curly."

This song is a great mood elevator, especially on a not-so-beautiful morning, when the irony of the situation brings a special smile to people sharing this song.

"LET IT SNOW! LET IT SNOW! LET IT SNOW!"

This 1946 recording was one of Vaughn Monroe's biggest vocal hits. The imperative "Let It Snow!" appears in the song nine times, so even if the group does not know the rest of the words, they do join in when the record reaches the line "Let It Snow! Let It Snow! Let It Snow!" Participants will be particularly amused if "Let It Snow!" is preceded by "Oh, What a Beautiful Morning!"

Because it is linked to the music it is associated with, music trivia can be the next best ice breaker to music itself. Brief oral quizzes about songs and singers, melodies and musicians can be combined with actual singing and discussion to initiate a little emotional release and provide a chance for some intellectual stimulation. The trick is to adapt the trivia questions to the particular group so that the older adults involved avoid frustration and experience success.

The following examples set a standard for the activity director, who can then proceed to create his or her own quizzes. (Written quizzes work only for older adults with good vision and unimpaired mental processes; for that reason we suggest that the following quizzes be given orally.) All quizzes can be made easier by adding clues. The answers are listed at the end of each quiz.

PERSONALITIES

1. What musical instrument did Jack Benny play? Did he play well?

2. Could you eat Carmen Miranda's hats? Why?

3. What animal did Latin bandleader Xavier Cugat carry in his tuxedo jacket pocket? What breed?

4. Ellington was the "Duke." Who was the "Count"?

5. Who called himself "The Vagabond Lover"?

6. What famous Italian-American started out as a vocalist for the Tommy Dorsey band?

7. What is Bing Crosby's biggest selling holiday song?

8. What famous "Doris" left Les Brown and His Band of Renown to become a far more famous movie star?

9. Artie Shaw, Woody Herman, and Benny Goodman all played the same musical instrument. What was it?

10. What bandleader called his radio show the College of Musical Knowledge?

ANSWERS

1) Violin; actually yes, but he pretended to play badly. 2) Yes; they were made of fruit. 3) Dog; chihuahua. 4) Count Basie. 5) Rudy Vallee. 6) Frank Sinatra. 7) "White Christmas." 8) Doris Day. 9) Clarinet. 10) Kay Kyser.

SONG TITLES

Where the blanks appear, say the word "blank" and encourage the group to replace the blank with the correct word. (After someone names the song, if he or she knows it, ask if he or she would be willing to sing it. If no one can answer, give a clue, a word, or the first letter of a word in the title until someone guesses.)

1. "Shine on _____ _____"
2. "I'm Forever _____ _____"
3. "Side by _____"
4. "_____ of New York"
5. "I'm Looking Over a _____ _____ _____"
6. "I'll Be Loving You _____"
7. "Accentuate the _____"
8. "Wait Till the Sun Shines _____"
9. "Oh, What a Beautiful _____"
10. "Gimme a Little _____, Will Ya, Huh?"

ANSWERS

1) Harvest Moon. 2) Blowing Bubbles. 3) Side. 4) Sidewalks. 5) Four-Leaf Clover. 6) Always. 7) Positive. 8) Nellie. 9) Morning. 10) Kiss.

BIG BANDS

1. "Sophisticated Lady" and "Take the 'A' Train" were popularized by _____.

2. This bandleader led a chorus called the Pennsylvanians. (He also invented the Waring Blender!)

3. "In the Mood," "Chattanooga Choo Choo," and "Moonlight Serenade" were all introduced by _____ _____.

4. Who was the "King of Swing?"

5. Who were the only two well-known brothers to form competing swing bands? (Hint: Their first names are Jimmy and Tommy.)

6. This bandleader-pianist knew how to make very few notes "count"; his theme song was "One O'Clock Jump." His last name rhymes with "spacey." Who was he?

7. Who led the Royal Canadians and played "Auld Lang Syne" at New York City's Roosevelt Hotel for more than 40 New Year's Eves?

8. Ziggy Elman, Louis Armstrong, and Harry James all played what musical instrument?

9. What band, whose theme was "Sentimental Journey," called itself the "Band of Renown"?

10. What bandleader deliberately broke instruments as well as played them and featured silly sound effects, including washboards and bicycle horns?

ANSWERS

1) Duke Ellington. 2) Fred Waring. 3) Glenn Miller. 4) Benny Goodman. 5) Dorsey. 6) Count Basie. 7) Guy Lombardo. 8) Trumpet. 9) Les Brown. 10) Spike Jones.

I CAN NAME
THAT TUNE
IN THREE NOTES

Remember the old television show called "Name That Tune"? Most older adults certainly do. If you are not a musician and cannot play the melody for the game, the second best way to do it is to play a tape of a familiar popular song. Play only a few seconds of the tape and see if anyone can guess the tune. Keep playing more of the song until someone guesses the correct song.

One of the best recordings available is called "Homecoming 1945" (Good Music Records, New York). The following songs are all from that recording, in the order in which they appear on the tapes, so it will not be necessary to skip around to find the selections. The delightful thing about this recording is that the songs are sung by the original artists; therefore, adults born in the 1920s and 1930s feel as if they are returning to their youth in a time machine when they listen to "Homecoming 1945."

1. "Shoo Fly Pie and Apple Pan Dowdy" (Dinah Shore)
2. "Moonlight Cocktail" (Glenn Miller)
3. "Twilight Time" (The Three Suns)
4. "Racing with the Moon" (Vaughn Monroe)
5. "Paper Doll" (The Mills Brothers)
6. "Dream" (The Pied Pipers)
7. "Is You Is or Is You Ain't My Baby?" (Bing Crosby)
8. "Bell Bottom Trousers" (Tony Pastor)
9. "All or Nothing at All" (Frank Sinatra)
10. "Till Then" (The Mills Brothers)

SONGS AND SINGERS

1. What perennial Christmas song did Gene Autry popularize?

2. What best-selling Christmas song of all time did Bing Crosby introduce in the movie *Holiday Inn?*

3. Who sang "You Made Me Love You" to a photograph of Clark Gable in the film *Broadway Melody of 1938?* She was 15 years old at the time.

4. What famous Monroe quit leading his band to become a multimillion-selling singer of such hits as "Red Roses for a Blue Lady" and "Ghost Riders in the Sky"?

5. What Lewis popularized the songs "When My Baby Smiles at Me" and "Me and My Shadow"?

6. What blackfaced minstrel man became world famous with his recordings of "Toot Toot Tootsie," "Mammy," and "Swanee"?

7. "Top Hat, White Tie and Tails," and "I Won't Dance" were written for what famous dancer?

8. What singer introduced the song "God Bless America"?

9. What famous female vocal trio recorded "Apple Blossom Time," "Pistol Packin' Mama," and "Boogie Woogie Bugle Boy"?

10. What male singer had hit recordings of "Blues in the Night," and "Minnie the Moocher"?

ANSWERS

1) "Rudolph the Red Nosed Reindeer." 2) "White Christmas." 3) Judy Garland. 4) Vaughn. 5) Ted. 6) Al Jolson. 7) Fred Astaire. 8) Kate Smith. 9) The Andrews Sisters. 10) Cab Calloway.

DRESS YOURSELF IN A SONG

All of the following song titles contain a blank space; fill in that blank with some item you can wear.

1. "Bell Bottom _____"
2. "Alice Blue _____"
3. "Button Up Your _____"
4. "Top Hat, White Tie and _____"
5. "Put on Your Old Gray _____"
6. "_____ Are a Girl's Best Friend"
7. "Silk _____"
8. "Buttons and _____"
9. "_____ Junction"
10. (You *put this on*, but you don't *really* wear it) "Puttin' On the _____"

ANSWERS

1) Trousers. 2) Gown. 3) Overcoat. 4) Tails. 5) Bonnet. 6) Diamonds. 7) Stockings. 8) Bows. 9) Tuxedo. 10) Ritz.

SONGS FROM MOVIES

1. Judy Garland sang this song in *The Wizard of Oz*.

2. In *Pinocchio*, Jiminy Cricket looked up at the night sky and sang what song?

3. In *Holiday Inn*, Bing Crosby introduced this Christmas song.

4. In Walt Disney's *Song of the South*, Uncle Remus sang this song, the title of which begins with the letter "Z."

5. Fernando Lamas and Esther Williams sang this song in *Neptune's Daughter* when she wanted to go and he wanted her to stay. Hint: First letter of title is "B."

6. Nat "King" Cole sang this song about a famous Leonardo Da Vinci painting.

7. In *The Jazz Singer*, Al Jolson sang this song about a father's love for his young son. Hint: First letter of the title is "S."

8. In *Rose Marie*, Nelson Eddy and Jeanette MacDonald sang this song of love. Hint: First word is "Indian."

9. In *Casablanca*, Humphrey Bogart and Ingrid Bergman listened to Dooley Wilson singing a love song whose title begins with the word "as."

10. In *The Harvey Girls*, Judy Garland and a large chorus that included Marjorie Main and Ray Bolger introduced a famous train song. Hint: The second word begins with the letter "A."

ANSWERS

1) "Over the Rainbow." 2) "When You Wish Upon a Star." 3) "White Christmas." 4) "Zip-a-Dee-Doo-Dah." 5) "Baby, It's Cold Outside." 6) "Mona Lisa." 7) "Sonny Boy." 8) "Indian Love Call." 9) "As Time Goes By." 10) "The Acheson, Topeka, and the Santa Fe."

PLANES, TRAINS, AND AUTOMOBILES

Fill in the blank in each title or first line of the following songs with a word that names some form of transportation.

LOOSE LIPS SINK SHIPS!

1. "Clang, Clang, Clang Went the _____"
2. "On a Slow _____ to China"
3. "_____ Built for Two"
4. "On the Good _____ Lollipop"
5. "In My Merry _____"
6. "Come Josephine In My _____ _____"
7. "I've Been Working on the _____"
8. "I'm Leaving on a _____ _____"
9. "Row, Row, Row Your _____"
10. "_____ with the Fringe on Top"

ANSWERS

1) Trolley. 2) Boat. 3) Bicycle. 4) Ship. 5) Oldsmobile. 6) Flying Machine. 7) Railroad. 8) Jet Plane. 9) Boat. 10) Surrey.

SONGS ABOUT PLACES

Fill in the blank in each title or first line of the following songs with a geographic location.

1. "Autumn in _____ _____"
2. "April in _____"
3. "Moonlight in _____"
4. "Moon Over _____"
5. "It's a Long Way to _____"
6. "I Love _____ in the Springtime"
7. "Pardon Me, Boy, Is That the _____ Choo Choo?"
8. "Give My Regards to _____"
9. "I Left My Heart in _____ _____"
10. (First line of song) "Why oh, why oh, why oh? Why did I ever leave _____?"

ANSWERS

1) New York. 2) Paris. 3) Vermont. 4) Miami. 5) Tipperary. 6) Paris. 7) Chattanooga. 8) Broadway. 9) San Francisco. 10) Ohio.

"MR." BILLIE HOLIDAY

When people think of the singer Billie Holiday, it is difficult not to think of the song "Lover Man"; it was her signature song. Yet, the song "Lover Man" nearly missed becoming part of Lady Day's repertoire.

In 1942 "Ram" Ramirez, one of the composers of "Lover Man," showed the song to Billie Holiday's manager, who rejected it, saying, "Billie's got too much class to sing this song."

Several months later, Ramirez heard about "Mr." Billie Holiday, a female impersonator who worked in a nightclub in Manhattan. When he went to see the man's act, he was shocked. Complete with gardenia in his black, chignoned hair, "Mr." Billie Holiday looked and sang like the real thing. After the show, Ramirez showed the female impersonator "Lover Man." The song impressed "Mr." Billie so much that he decided to make it a part of his act.

Later, Billie Holiday's manager was urged to see the female impersonator's act. When he heard "Mr." Billie sing "Lover Man," he immediately knew it was perfect for his client.

Not long afterward, Holiday's manager gave her a copy of "Lover Man," which she made a point of singing at nearly every performance. Her manager did not discover until later that the song he had loved instantly was also the song he had previously rejected.

EUBIE BLAKE'S SONGWRITING SECRET

Back in the 1920s, Eubie Blake wrote dozens of melodies to accompany the lyrics of his partner, Noble Sissle. While they were writing songs for the Broadway show *Blackbirds of 1930*, Sissle asked Blake, "When are you gonna write a *new* tune?"

"I'm working on it now," Blake replied.

Sissle exclaimed, "No, you're not! You change a few notes here and there, but, for the most part, you've been using the same tune for every lyric I write."

When Blake looked back over his songs, he was shocked to discover that Sissle was right. He was determined to create a melody that was *completely* original. This is how Eubie Blake said he did it: "I got the melody out of the phone book, let the numbers stand for notes of the scale, and zero stood for 'C.' Well, what I found was 455, 566, 602, 41; and I turned that into G-A-A, A-B-B, B-C-E, G-D."

The melody Eubie Blake found in the telephone book became the song "Memories of You." When Blake was in his late 90s, he said, "My publisher made me promise never to tell this story, but I'm old now, and I don't see it's right that I die with the secret." So, "Memories of You" was written by Eubie Blake, with a little help from "Ma Bell."

STAGE DIRECTIONS THAT INSPIRED A SONG LYRIC

In the early years of the Broadway theatre, shows were supposed to open with a lively chorus of beautiful women, but Rodgers and Hammerstein's *Oklahoma* opened in 1943 with a lone man on an empty stage singing a gentle song.

The opening scene in *Oklahoma* grew out of the stage directions in Lynn Riggs' *Green Grow the Lilacs*, the stage play on which *Oklahoma* is based. Oscar Hammerstein read the following lines: "It is a radiant summer morning several years ago…cattle, corn, streams… seem to exist now for the first time, their images giving off a visible golden emana-

tion," and thought it was a shame to waste such beautiful imagery on stage directions that a theater audience would never read or hear. Hammerstein transformed the stage directions into the lyrics of the song "Oh, What a Beautiful Morning."

> There's a bright golden haze on the meadow…
> The corn is as high as an elephant's eye,
> And it looks like it's climbing clear up to the sky!

FOLK MUSIC MEETS TIN PAN ALLEY

In the 1930s bluesman Leadbelly (Huddie Ledbetter) was attacked by a patron in a bar. In order to defend himself, he stabbed his opponent to death. He was convicted of murder and spent the next few years behind bars, where he passed the time creating songs on his 12-string guitar. John Lomax, the folklorist, heard about Leadbelly and arranged for him to be signed to a recording contract while still in prison. Although Leadbelly never had much commercial success, young folksingers idolized the blues singer and played his songs, especially one called "Goodnight Irene."

In the 1940s Pete Seeger, Erik Darling, Lee Hayes, and Fred Hellerman formed a folk quartet called the Almanac Singers. They had known Leadbelly, and they featured his songs in their concerts.

By the end of the 1940s record executives thought that using large orchestras and choruses in the background might help folk music appeal to a larger audience. Bandleader-arranger Gordon Jenkins hired the Almanac Singers, who had since changed their name to the Weavers, and arranged for them to sing "Goodnight Irene" with a large studio orchestra. This marked the beginning of commercial folk music, which would later make Harry Belafonte; the Kingston Trio; and Peter, Paul, and Mary internationally famous.

Gordon Jenkins and the Weavers' 1950 single "Goodnight Irene" stayed on the hit parade for 15 weeks. The song sold 2 million recordings that first year. Folk music would never be the same again.

THE WIZARD OF THE GUITAR

In 1928 the man who was to become one of the greatest guitarists of his generation was a high school student in Waukesha, Wisconsin. Already a talented musician, Les Paul played acoustic guitar and sang on weekends at Beekman's Barbecue Stand, where waitresses walked between cars to take food orders and people ate in their cars as they listened to young Les' music.

People enjoyed the music, but complained that they could not hear him play anything clearly except his harmonica. After giving the problem some thought, Paul brought his mother's Kolster console radio to Beekman's. He removed the bell-shaped mouthpiece from the family telephone, attached it to a broom handle, and strung a wire from the broom handle to the radio speaker. Voila! Les Paul had invented what was probably the world's first portable public address (P.A.) system.

Alas, the crowds at the barbecue stand could not hear Les' guitar nearly as well as his singing. The teenager returned to Beekman's the following weekend with a second invention. This time he borrowed his father's Atwater Kent radio, which was kept in the family's garage. He detached the family phonograph pickup, including the needle, which he jammed into the body of his $4.50 Sears Roebuck guitar, and connected the pickup to the Atwater Kent radio speaker via a wire. After a few initial squeals, the sound of the guitar emerged loudly and clearly from the speaker. Thirteen-year-old Les Paul had created the world's first electric guitar!

AIN'T THAT PERFECTION?

Jack Yellen wrote one of the top 10 hits of the 1920s and made tens of thousands of dollars from it. Yellen retired in the early 1950s, to his farm in Springville, New York. One day he opened the mailbox to find a letter from a place he had not visited in 40 years—his hometown. Inside the envelope was an invitation to his 40th high school class reunion.

Yellen decided to add a little celebrity to the class reunion by attending. When he arrived, the town was hardly recognizable and the crowded gymnasium was full of unfamiliar faces. Suddenly, he felt that someone was staring at him from across the room. He glanced over and saw a woman leaning on a cane. She must be close to 90 years old, Yellen thought. As he looked more closely at the woman, he finally recognized his high school English teacher.

She moved toward him and asked, "Jack, is that you?"

He said, "Yes, ma'am."

She asked, "Did you write that song?"

Because he'd written many songs, he asked, "What song?"

She clenched her teeth and said, "'Ain't... she...sweet!'"

Yellen said, "Yes, ma'am, I wrote it."

His former teacher demanded, reproachfully, "Didn't I teach you that *ain't* was bad grammar?"

With a sheepish grin on his face, Yellen answered, "Yeah, but it was good money!"

THERE'S GOLD IN THEM THAR DISCS!

Wes Abel, a former student at the Peabody Conservatory Elderhostel in Baltimore, spent 10 years in the employ of RCA Victor in charge of record mastering. Wes explained that gold records were, at that time, a necessary part of the recording process because gold, being the most malleable metal, is best able to retain the minute gradations in ways that result in clearer reproduction. However, several gold record masters were made of a popular disc because the softness of gold metal caused it to wear out eventually. The black plastic discs sold to the public were manufactured by pouring the semiliquid plastic over the gold disc, pressing it, and peeling it off when it dried to a hard plastic.

Abel explained that histories of popular music refer to the record industry's decision to award gold discs to its million-selling artists. However, according to him, the first gold record award was actually given as a prank. In 1948 Vaughn Monroe sold 1 million copies of "Dance, Ballerina, Dance." He was coming into the studio to record on his birthday, and Abel and a few of the RCA executives thought it might be fun to celebrate his birthday. They sent a secretary to the five and ten to buy a tiny plastic ballerina with a lace tutu, which they mounted on the center of a gold record. When Monroe walked through the door he saw the gold record and the little ballerina on the turntable. When the men set the record spinning, the ballerina appeared to dance. They all wished Monroe a happy birthday and presented him with the gold record and the tiny ballerina.

Abel says that when other million-selling artists heard about the informal event, they demanded to know why *they* had not been given gold records. So, at RCA Victor, all million-selling artists soon began receiving gold records. Within 2 years, the entire record industry followed RCA's lead.

A MUSICAL LOVE STORY

Clarence MacKay sent his daughter Ellin on a cruise to Europe to separate her from the man she loved, composer Irving Berlin. MacKay kept Ellin's itinerary a secret and even intercepted her letters to cut off communication between the two, but Berlin was not about to give up Ellin MacKay.

Berlin knew that Ellin, wherever she was, would turn the radio on from time to time. When she did, she would hear the announcer say, "Here's a song by Irving Berlin," and suddenly the room would be filled with music: "What'll I do when you are far away, and I am blue? What'll I do?" He knew she would hear his new song: "All alone, by the telephone, wondering where you are, and how you are, and if you are all alone, too."

Berlin's hunch was right. Filled with the emotion of her lover's songs, Ellin MacKay returned to America to marry Berlin. However, her father was not easily beaten, and, according to Alexander Woolcott, Berlin's first biographer, MacKay said, "I'll give you 1 million dollars to leave my daughter alone."

Unruffled, Berlin replied. "I'll give you 2 million to leave *me* alone!" He left to meet Ellin at the gangplank with a song-sheet in his hand, a wedding present to his bride-to-be (the copyright was in her name). The song was called "(I'll Be Loving You) Always."

All of the preceding songs, quizzes, and anecdotes have been tailored to be successful with groups of older adults with various cognitive abilities, which, particularly in adult day care centers and long-term care facilities, tend to be the types of groups with which an activity director works. Music is so basic and common a bond that the distinction that alert participants make between themselves and participants with cognitive disabilities vanishes as the entire group shares and enjoys music activities together.

The Power of Music Audiocassette

Vocals Fran Mahr and Bill Messenger
Piano, Narration Bill Messenger • *French Horn* Sean Finn

Side 1   Action Songs
1   Low Down Blues (piano)
2   Bingo (vocal)
3   You Must Come in at the Door (vocal)
4   Theme from *The New World Symphony* (French horn)
5   Shoo Fly (vocal)
6   Twinkle, Twinkle Little Star (vocal)
7   Take Me Out to the Ball Game (piano)
8   Put Your Hand in the Air (vocal)
9   The Missouri Waltz (piano)
10   Jitterboogie (piano)
11   This Is the Way (vocal)
12   Looby Lou (vocal)
13   Mary Ann McCarthy (vocal)
14   Mama Don't 'Low (vocal)
15   The Rachmaninoff Rag (piano)
16   The Entertainer (piano)

Side 2   Songs for Successful Sing-Alongs
1   Daisy Bell
2   By the Light of the Silvery Moon
3   Take Me Out to the Ball Game
4   Amazing Grace
5   Ja-Da
6   After the Ball
7   Oh! Susanna
8   The Sidewalks of New York
9   Swing Low, Sweet Chariot
10   Aba Daba Honeymoon
11   Shine On, Harvest Moon
12   You're A Grand Old Flag
13   Peg O' My Heart
14   Meet Me in St. Louis, Louis
15   I Want A Girl
16   Yankee Doodle Boy
17   America, the Beautiful
18   School Days
19   For Me and My Gal
20   Let Me Call You Sweetheart
21   After You've Gone (piano)